decadence 27

Nietzsche 42

Correspondence Across a Room

Vyacheslav Ivanovich Ivanov
and
Mikhail Osipovich Gershenzon

CORRESPONDENCE
ACROSS A ROOM

Translated by Lisa Sergio

THE MARLBORO PRESS
MARLBORO, VERMONT
1984

Originally published in Russian as PEREPISKA IZ DVNUKH UGLOV.

Manufactured in the United States of America
Library of Congress Catalog Card Number 84-60897
ISBN 0-910395-11-X

Translator's Note

The original Russian edition of these twelve letters was published in Petrograd in 1921. Another Russian-language edition appeared in Berlin in 1922; then, in 1926, a German translation was printed in the January issue of *Die Kreatur*. The French translation printed in 1930 in the review *Vigile* was brought out in book form the following year with a preface by G. Michel and a letter from Ivanov to Charles du Bos (Paris: Corréa). An Italian translation made by Olga Resnevic was published in 1932 (Lanciano: Carabba Editori). A Dutch translation was published in the late 1930's and a Czech version appeared in Prague in 1960. An English version appeared in the September, 1949 *Partisan Review*.

For their careful reading of the present translation and for their suggestions, my grateful thanks are owing to Professor Vadim Melish and Mark Melish.

—Lisa Sergio

CORRESPONDENCE ACROSS A ROOM

I. *To M.O. Gershenzon*

I KNOW, dear friend and neighbor across the way in this room we share, that you are assailed by doubts about personal immortality and about the existence of a personal God. I am hardly sure I am fitted to plead man's right to metaphysical status and elevation because, in truth, I find nothing within myself that can lay claim to eternal life. Nothing, at any rate, except that something which is not myself but a common and universal part of me which, a radiant visitor, illuminates my finite, precarious being with spiritual light. Nonetheless it would seem to me that it is not for nothing that this guest has come and "taken up his abode in me." I believe that, in return for my hospitality, his purpose is to bring his host the gift of an immortality my reason cannot comprehend. My personal being is immortal not through the fact of its existence but because it heeds a call to wake into existence. Like every awakening, like my own coming into this world, it partakes of the miraculous.

I see clearly that in my own personality and in all of

its countless manifestations, there is not one atom that comes anywhere near to the barest notion of autonomous and true being, that is, eternal being.

I am a seed lying dead in the earth; but "if the seed dieth not, how shall it return to life again?" God will raise me up again because God is within me. I know Him in me as a dark birthing place; I know Him in me as the eternal fount of what in me is best and holiest; I know Him in me as the living principle of being, more inclusive than myself, and containing, along with the other qualities that make me up, the quality of personal consciousness distinctive in me. I have emerged from Him and He abides in me. If He does not leave me He will also create in me other forms of His continuing presence in me, that is to say, my own person. God has not merely created me, you see, He is creating me without cease and will continue to create me in the future because He desires me to create Him in myself in the future as He has created me up until the present.

There can be no such descent of God without a voluntary accepting of Him, for, in a sense, these two acts have equal value: he who receives becomes equal in dignity to him who bestows. God cannot abandon me if I do not abandon Him. The law of love, graven in our hearts—where we can read its invisible characters without difficulty—assures us that the Psalmist was right when he said to the Lord: "Thou wilt not leave my soul in hell; neither wilt thou suffer Thine Holy One to see corruption."

This, my dear neighbor, is what I am thinking in my corner, since you wished to know. And you, what will you reply from over there in yours?

—V.I.

June 17, 1920

II. *To V.I. Ivanov*

No, V.I., I do not doubt personal immortality; like you, I consider the individual person to be the repository of true reality. But these are things, it seems to me, about which we should not talk or even think. We two, my dear friend, are at the opposite ends of the diagonal, not just in this room, but in spirit also. I do not much like to hoist my thoughts up to the high realm of metaphysics, although I enjoy seeing you take such effortless flight there. These speculations inevitably harden into systems governed by laws of logic; this building of castles in the air, which many of the people in our circle are addicted to, strikes me as idle and pointless. All this abstraction oppresses me, furthermore, and not the abstraction alone, for in recent times all the intellectual conquests of mankind, all the wealth of concepts, knowledge and values collected and classified throughout the centuries have become—for me—an onerous burden, like garments too heavy and too encumbering to wear. In the past this feeling would trouble me only now and then; of late, however, it has become constant so that I look ahead

4

fondly to plunging into some Lethe that would leave my memory cleansed of every religious or philosophical system; every trace of wisdom, of doctrine, of the arts and of poetry would be gone from my soul; and returning naked to the bank, as the first man was naked, light and joyous, I could lift my arms toward the sky, remembering one thing only out of the past: how tight and stifling were those garments and how free I feel without them! Why all this has taken hold of me I do not know. Perhaps when the garments were new and intact and well-fitted to our bodies, we were not aware of them as a burden. But now that they are tattered and hang down in rags our one thought is to be rid of them forever.

—M.G.

III. *To M.O. Gershenzon*

I AM not a builder of systems, dear M.O., but neither am I one of those frightened persons who scent a lie behind everything that is said. I am accustomed to wandering in the "forest of symbols" and I understand the symbolism of a word as readily as I understand that of a kiss. To inner experience there corresponds a verbal form which it must achieve or else wither, its meaning unexpressed. We must take good care, however, not to frame these communications in compulsive language, placing them, that is, under the authority of reason. For reason is compulsive by nature, whereas the spirit breathes where it lists. To convey inner experience words must be spiritual words, spirit-born, truly the offspring of freedom. Even as the song of the poet moves us but does not compel us, so words ought to move the mind of him who listens rather than imposing acquiescence upon him, as to a proven theorem.

Metaphysics has fallen prey to pride and the thirst for power, tragically so, and as a consequence of separating itself from the matrix of spiritual knowledge.

6

Primitive religion was its original home: leaving it, metaphysics must sooner or later undertake to reshape itself along scientific lines, and strive to secure the scepter of the mighty despot that is science itself. The state of mind that now torments you, your exasperated intolerance of the cultural heritage you feel weighing upon you, stems essentially from the fact that you experience culture, not as a living repertory of gifts, but as a subtle mechanism of multiple compulsions. And this is not surprising, culture having indeed sought to become a system of compulsions. For my part I see it as a ladder of Eros, a hierarchy of acts of veneration. So many are the things and persons I am moved to venerate, beginning with man and his tools and his labors and his insulted dignity and ending with the lowliest bit of mineral, that I find it sweet to go down in this sea—*naufragar mi è dolce in questo mare*—, to drown in God. My acts of veneration are freely consented, none are imposed or extorted, their objects are open and accessible, my soul rejoices in each of them. Yet each act of veneration, as it turns into love, with love's penetrating eye discerns the inner tragedy and tragic guilt within every object that has cut itself off from the source of all being and exists isolated in itself: there beneath every rose of life lies the reminder of the cross it flowered from. But this too is the yearning for God, the yearning of the moth-like soul for the flame that will consume it. This is a fundamental yearning, and he who is a stranger to it, says Goethe, is sick with another desire. Though he may maintain an unfalter-

7

ing mask of gaiety, behind it he is a "gloomy visitor upon the dark earth." Our true freedom, at once our noblest happiness and our noblest suffering, is always with us and no culture can take it away. However, while the spirit is valiant, the flesh is not. Against destitution and disease a man cannot put up as brave a front as against broken idols. Violence will not enable him to be rid of the hated yoke of a deadening tradition, for it will grow back again of its own accord, just as the camel's hump is still there after he has flung off the burden on his back. The spirit does not free itself from this yoke otherwise than by taking on another, "the yoke that is light." With good cause you berate the man who is a slave to his riches: "Become!" (*Werde*), you enjoin him, but you are forgetting Goethe's condition: "die first"—*stirb und werde.* Death whereby he is reborn is the liberation for which man yearns. Bathe yourself in living waters, and be consumed in fire. This is possible this very morning, or any morning, as the spirit awakens every day.

—V.I.

June 19, 1920

IV. *To V.I. Ivanov*

OUR accidentally started correspondence from corner to corner is beginning to interest me. You will remember how when I was absent once, you wrote the
first letter and left it on my table as you were on your
way out. I answered it, in turn, while you were away.
Now I write in your presence, while you are silently
concentrated upon ironing out the stubborn age-old
wrinkles in Dante's verses with a view to reshaping
them into Russian. By writing to you my thoughts
will gain in fullness and ring clearer, like a sound
heard within a great silence. After dinner we shall
again lie each on his bed, you with a sheet of paper and
I with a small leather-bound book, you will read aloud
your translation of *Purgatory*, the results of your
morning's work, while I compare it with the original
text and offer criticisms. And again today, as on other
recent days, I shall imbibe the rich mead of your poetry, and as I do that familiar distress shall once again
revive in me.

Ah, my friend, swan of Apollo! Why was feeling so
vibrant, thought so fresh and words so charged with

meaning in the fourteenth century, and why are our thoughts and feelings today so pallid and our speech so covered with cobwebs? Rightly indeed have you spoken of metaphysics as a system of barely perceptible compulsions; but it is of something else I am speaking. I am speaking of our culture as a whole and of its subtle emanations that have spread like a stain throughout the entire fabric of existence. I speak not of compulsions but of temptations that have disintegrated, weakened, and distorted our minds. No, it is something beyond this I am speaking of, something beyond the consequences of culture and the harm it does, for the evaluation of the gains and losses accruing from culture is reason's affair—and every argument that wields the sword will perish by it too. Are we to trust our intellect in this matter when we know with certainty that this reason of ours derives from culture and worships culture as naturally as an undistinguished slave prostrates himself before the master who has improved his lot?

Another judge, an incorruptible one, has also spoken up within me. Perhaps because I was weary of a burden become too heavy for me, perhaps because something of my original mind strove through the clutter there of knowledge and habit—whatever the cause, a simple, unmistakable feeling has risen and established itself inside me, as emphatic as the feeling of hunger or pain. I am not passing judgment on culture. I am merely attesting the fact that I feel suffocated by it. As did Rousseau, I dream of a state of bliss—no worldly cares, a complete freedom of spirit, a paradise. I know too much, and what I know weighs upon me. This is not knowledge acquired by me through personal experience; its origin is general and foreign, it is knowledge inherited from forefathers and ancestors. With its allurements of demonstrability it has won entrance into my mind and taken it over. Precisely because it is general, impersonally demonstrated, it is indisputable, and its indisputability freezes my soul. Proven facts by the million, so many unbreakable threads, imprison me in their net. They are impersonal facts, immutable, inescapable—horrible. And of what use are all these proven facts to me? In most cases, of none. I do not need them in love or in sorrow, it is not through their help that, amidst grave errors and unexpected successes, I grope toward an understanding of my destiny. It is not them I shall recall in my final hour. Like trash they litter my mind. Every minute of my life, they hang like a dusty curtain between me and my happiness, my pain and my aspirations. From this ocean of impersonal knowledge, from these countless concepts stamped into our memories, from the truths, the hypotheses, the rules of logic and the moral laws, from this immense heap of intellectual riches every one of us is laden with, from all this, I say, comes the exhaustion that devours us.

Just let me recall to you the theory of the thing in itself and of the phenomenon. The great Kant discovered that we know nothing of the thing itself, that our representations of it are as close as we can get to it.

11

Schopenhauer drove this truth further home by demonstrating that we are completely enclosed within ourselves, with no way of getting beyond the confines of our consciousness or making contact with the world. The thing in itself is unknowable: in perceiving the world we only perceive phenomena and the laws under which our intellect operates. We only imagine the outside world, or dream it, it does not exist at all, and our perception apparatus is the only reality. This discovery was logically irrefutable. The truth shone forth with overwhelming force, and our thinking has to yield to it unquestioningly. In men's minds the greatest revolution took place; things, people, I myself as a creature, all tangible reality, once solid, now suddenly rose a foot above the ground, turned into an apparition. Nothing remained but mirages, created according to laws, with which our spirit, God knows why, chose to fill the void.

The doctrine held sway for one hundred years, deeply influencing our thinking. Finally, however, without our even being aware, it began to lose power, dimmed, and finally died. Philosophers have dared rise to the defense of the naive experience of the past and a reality of undoubted solidity has been restored to the external world, while little but a tiny particle of the once blinding discovery has survived: the truth perceived by Kant that the formal aspects of our cognition—time, space and causality—are strictly ideal, inherent, not in the world, but in our consciousness and laid by the latter upon our experience, much as a network of markings is laid down upon a map. The old illusion had vanished, but how terrible are the traces that survive! The nightmare of unreality still enfolds reason in a web of madness. Man is returning slowly and with much hesitancy to the cognizance of reality, much as a convalescent recovering from a long illness fears that everything around him may be a dream. Thus abstract reasoning in the laboratories of science evolves systems and theories which, though infallible for science, are alien to our spirit. The day these so-called truths begin to fall apart, as they inevitably must, we ask ourselves sadly: Why did they swaddle our minds and hamper its movements for so many years? Just as goods on display in shops tempt us with their attractive appearance and promise of usefulness, so do ideas and knowledge proffer vacuous temptations until our spirit becomes as overloaded with them as our homes are stuffed with superfluous and useless objects. Ideas and knowledge are fruitful only if they are naturally born of personal experience. But when acquired second-hand, from the outside, corresponding to no natural need, it is like the starched collars, rubber overshoes, umbrellas and pocket watches that a native of the African jungle uses to adorn his nakedness after bartering them from a European. This is why I say the proliferation of man-made wares cluttering my house annoys me, but the excess baggage weighing on my spirit is far worse. I would give all the thoughts and the knowledge I have culled from books, as well as everything I have built on top of them, for the sheer joy of achieving spontaneously, through my own experience, just one piece of simple knowledge, fresh as a summer morning.

And, I repeat, the crux of it all is not the compulsiveness you have dwelled upon, but the temptation. Temptation is more compulsive than violence. Abstract reasoning, holding out the temptation of objective truth, forces its findings upon us. You say that were we to cast off the burden we should begin to accumulate it again and become burdened anew. Agreed: we can neither rid ourselves of our reasoning nor alter its nature. Yet I know of and consider possible another upsurge of creativity and another culture that will be able to forego transforming every last cognition into dogma, every blessing into a desiccated mummy, every value into a fetish. Obviously, it's not I all by myself but many others as well who are suffocating within these walls of stone. And you, a poet, would you have been able to adapt to living here without protest if fate had not bestowed upon you the gift of inspiration by which, at least for a time, you escape the walls on wings of song, soaring into the open and into the realm of the soul? With envy my eyes follow your flights and the flights of other poets: space exists and man has wings! Yet, my eyes perceive other things too—is it their fault? They see that the wings of Apollo's swans no longer carry them to great heights. How, I ask you, in this era of enlightenment, how is the poet to preserve the power and freshness of his native inspiration? At the age of thirty, he has today read so many books and discussed so many philosophies that he is saturated by the abstract intellectualism of his milieu.

And now I must answer your final plea. The liberation of personality, the true liberation you speak of at the end, the *Flammentod* of Goethe, is also an *élan* and a flight of the spirit, similar to the inspiration of poets but infinitely more daring and resolute. This is why these occurrences are rare in our time, rarer even than works of genius in the arts. The "cultural heritage" weighs upon the personality with the weight of sixty atmospheres and more, but because of its temptations it is a yoke that lies lightly. The majority are not even conscious it is there; but he who does feel it and would resist it—oh, just let him try to leap free of its massive grip! For it does not only lie upon our shoulders, it is within us. Man himself has become heavy. Only the wings of genius can hope to lift his spirit above his burdened consciousness.

—M.G.

V. *To M.O. Gershenzon*

MY dear friend, we are living in the same cultural milieu, in the same room, each of us in his own corner, but there is only one window and only one door. At the same time, each of us has his own home which both you and I would gladly exchange for a place under a different sky. But living in the same milieu does not mean the same thing for all its inhabitants and guests. In a given element, such as the sea, there are soluble substances and there are also oil, algae and coral, pearl-bearing shells and whales, flying fish and dolphins, amphibious creatures as well as men diving for pearls.

It appears to me—unless my eyes deceive me—that you are unable to conceive of living in a culture without becoming one with it. My position, on the contrary, is that consciousness can indeed be of a piece with culture, and that it also can be partly immanent to culture and partly transcendent. And this is easily shown, by the way, with the following example, which is especially relevant to our discussion. A man who believes in God would never agree that his faith is part of culture, whereas a man imprisoned within the confines of culture will inevitably regard faith as a phenomenon of culture regardless of how he defines its nature: as historically conditioned psychology, as heritage, as poetry or metaphysics, as a sociological force, or even as a moral value. Such a man can define faith however you please so long as he ends up including it among cultural phenomena. He will never agree with the believer that faith exists apart from the sphere of culture, is autonomous, simple, primordial and links the individual self to the Absolute Being. The believer sees his faith as essentially separate from culture, the way love or nature are separate from it.

Thus it is from our faith in the Absolute—which is not culture—that we derive our inner freedom, which is life itself; whilst from a lack of faith derives our enslavement to culture, a culture that has been essentially godless ever since (as Kant made so clear) it left man a prisoner within his own self. Only through faith, the disavowal of the original sin of culture, can the temptations of culture, of which you are so keenly aware, be overcome.

Original sin, however, cannot be eradicated simply by destroying the outward forms of sin. If one were to unlearn how to write or, following Plato, if we banished the Muses, these would only be palliatives: letters would reappear in due course, the scrolls would again proclaim the unalterable story of the captives chained to the rock in Plato's cave. Rousseau's dream arose out of his unbelief: to live in God means not to live entirely within the relativity of human culture, but to grow in an outward direction from it towards freedom with some part of one's being.

Life in God is life become real: it is movement, it is spiritual growth, the upward path, the ladder heavenward. We need but set forth: where we put our feet, there the path will be—the rest will follow. Surrounding things will give way of themselves, voices will recede, great new horizons will open up. The gateway out to freedom is the same for all who live within the same enclosure, and it is always open. If one man goes forth, another is likely to follow and perhaps, one after another, all will eventually step beyond the threshold. Without faith in God mankind cannot retrieve the freshness of spirit it has lost. It does not suffice to discard old garments, it is the old Adam one must discard. Only the water of life rejuvenates. The seductive image now before you of a renewed community without Muses and the written word is only a delusion, a sign of decadence as is all Rousseauism, unless the new human community of your vision, severed from its traditional culture, becomes a community of prayer. Otherwise this new shoot of humanity will soon show itself to come from the same corrupt branch as we.

If you reply that a new dispensation of culture is already under way, that the new signs being inscribed on the *tabula rasa* of the human soul will guarantee mankind a revitalized creative power, a new perception of the world, a new youth for many years to come, I can have but one reaction: to shrug my shoulders and wonder greatly at the optimism of such an answer, proceeding as it does from the failure—characteristic of Rousseau's age—to comprehend the fatal truth, that the wellsprings of spiritual life have been poisoned, that the Orphic or Biblical assertion of original sin is not, alas, a falsehood. In such a case our conversation would be reminiscent of that other in Plato's *Timaeus*, where the interlocutors were Solon and an Egyptian priest. "O Solon, Solon, you Hellenes are never anything but children," says the priest, "and there is not an old man among you." He goes on to say that floods and fires have again and again ravaged the world, but after each of these devastations the people who dwelt in the land of the Hellenes were reborn "without Muses and without writings" in order to rebuild their unenduring works yet another time, while immobile Egypt, always saved by the sacred waters of the Nile, preserved in its millenarian registers the memory of ancient forefathers forgotten by the Hellenes, the great and glorious race of men who once threw off the yoke of remote Atlantis.

My dear fellow-interlocutor, like the Egyptian and his Greek disciple, and like Plato himself, I devoutly burn my incense on the altar of Memory, mother of the Muses. I celebrate her as the "promise of immortality" and the "crown of consciousness" and am convinced that no upward step may be taken on the ladder of spiritual ascent without also taking a step downward in that underground direction where the

19

sources of the spirit are—for, as you know, the higher the branches, the deeper the roots.

And if in rebuttal you were to say that you did not intend or feel entitled to predict what the attitudes of the people of the new culture will be, that you simply feel, for yourself and your progeny, an overwhelming need to emerge from this asphyxiating dungeon into the open air, without knowing or wishing to know what you or they are apt to encounter beyond the prison walls, you would be expressing a fatalistic indifference towards the task of carving out the paths to freedom and an ultimate despair of your own liberation. Let it not be so!

—V.I.

June 30, 1920

VI. *To V.I. Ivanov*

KINDEST and dearest neighbor, these tender inducements to leave my corner and come into yours are in vain. Walls surround your corner, too, and it is devoid of freedom. Let the man of culture but surrender himself to faith, you say, and he is already essentially free. I reply: weighted down by his cultural heritage, he is incapable of rising to the Absolute. Even if he has faith, his faith, like his other spiritual states, is affected by reflection, reflection distorts and renders it impotent. I repeat what I wrote to you the last time: our consciousness cannot transcend culture, or can do so only on the rarest, most exceptional occasions. Witness the strugglings of our friend Shestov. How often we have spoken affectionately of him! Will he not come to see the emptiness of speculation, the crippling dogmatism of ideas and systems? Does he not long for freedom? His unhappy spirit struggles helplessly to break free. He strives to undo the knots of dogmatic thought that pinion mankind, he enthusiastically relates the momentary victories of a Nietzsche or Dostoevski, or of an Ibsen or Tolstoy—and then come the

21

lamentable stories of their return to the kennel. One cannot achieve freedom when there is poison in the bloodstream and exhaustion in the bones. Our faith, love and inspiration, all the things in us that can liberate the spirit . . . in us are infected and sick. How can you conceive of giant oaks or tender violets sprouting from a soil littered with the remains of ancient systems and concepts, with the wreckage of ancient structures, with, scattered amidst the rest, mausoleums containing undying and undisputed spiritual values, those of art, faith or thought? Nothing could grow upon such soil except miserable scrub or the ivy that thrives on ruins.

But this is not what I meant to talk about. You are right: I neither know nor want to know what may be encountered beyond the prison walls; as for the cause of "carving out paths to freedom," that, frankly, leaves me cold. For this, my friend, is speculation, once again speculation. I already have enough with the speculation that permeates the air around me and invades my reason. Ratiocinations do not interest me anymore. I "simply" feel, as you say, a vital need of freedom for my spirit and my consciousness, quite as, I would suppose, a sixth century Greek probably felt, smothering within the enveloping multiplicity of the gods on his Olympus, their diverse qualities and claims, the profusion of sanctified myths and religious rituals, and quite as some Australian aborigine is probably suffocating at this moment in the cloying atmosphere of his bewildering animism or totemism, lacking the strength necessary to liberate himself from them. Perhaps within him the imprisoned Greek dreamed of an outside where he would stand before a single, universal, impersonal God, of whom there were intimations in his spirit; perhaps that Australian dreams of the spirit's ease beyond the oppressions of fear, dreams of being free to choose a spouse beyond the taboos imposed by totemistic law. But neither one nor the other would know how to give positive expression to his dreams and longings.

He who seeks liberation sees only what stands in the way of it and gives voice only to his negation; but his struggling and negating is always "in the name" of something, a positive ideal has already come into being within him, and upon it he draws for the passion and the strength to carry on the fight. Vague and unexpressed, it is yet the only kind of ideal that rouses the will. Conversely, an ideal clearly apprehended and clearly expressed shortly disintegrates into a system of ideas, circumscribed by reason, diminished, too feeble to engage the will.

What do I want? I want freedom of consciousness and of inquiry, I want the primordial youthfulness of spirit to venture where I wish, along unbroken paths, first because this would give me pleasure and second because—who knows?—new paths might well lead to further discovery. But no: the main reason is that it is boring where we are, as it is in our sanitorium. I long for the fields and the forests.

Not only do I wish for this freedom, but I am convinced that it will come. How else account for this feeling in me? The authenticity and intensity of my feeling assure me that this will come about. From reptiles, you know, came the birds, and that burning and itching on the amphibian's shoulders where his wings were about to sprout is just what I feel. The confused dreams of that Greek and Australian were auguries of the freedom that comes centuries later. Perhaps after his original freedom man had to go through a long period of discipline, restrained by laws and dogmas, before re-emerging into the new freedom we speak of. It could be. But pity those generations whose destiny was to live in the intermediate stage, the stage of culture.

Culture is disintegrating—disintegrating within our very selves, where it hangs in tatters from our exhausted spirits. Whether this will prove the form liberation takes or whether it will coincide with some catastrophe, as it did twenty centuries ago, I cannot tell. I shall certainly not reach the Promised Land, but my feeling for it is like being on Mount Nebo where Moses beheld it from afar. And I am not alone in perceiving it through a veil of thunderclouds.

—M.O.

VII. *To M.O. Gershenzon*

"THERE is no motion," quoth the bearded sage; his interlocutor rejoined with the symbolic advice that he verify his opinion by means of a practical test, and with that the sage began to walk about in front of him. The sage was not a cripple, he too could move his legs. But to this he attached no value, because he did not believe in his own experience. I attribute most of your objections to auto-suggestion, to the impact of preconceived ideas of a speculative order, even less warranted than the sage's denial that motion existed in the use of his legs.

Another part of your objections, I believe, stems from your unslaked thirst for life. There is much despair in your words and between the lines, in the rhythm and resonance within those words, and in the vitality that is characteristic of you there is so much youthful vigor, so much eagerness to try the untried, to strike out along unexplored paths, to confidently embrace nature, there is so much longing for adventure and for the new that the generous earth holds in store—*tant de désir, enfin, de faire un peu l'école*

25

buissonnière—that it seems to me, dear Doctor Faustus reincarnate, that Mephistopheles, contemplating you, could hope for success were he but able to hit upon the right temptations with which to draw forth into a broad and free existence one who, tired of carrying the burden of his faculties, has barricaded himself in the corner he withdrew into. Needless to say, with you Mephisto would have to employ artifices subtler by far than the vision of a feminine form appearing in the magical distance. More appropriate would be a vision of flowers in a meadow, or of a lovely glade in an unspoiled wood, after a little reminder that theory is grey while the tree of life is forever green.

Obviously, too, that inviting freedom yonder, the new adventures once over with, would reveal itself a dead end, another prison. The last of the temptations undergone by Faust would, in your case, probably be the first: the canals, the new world, the illusions of a free land for the free people. There is no limit, is there, to the number of two-dimensional constructions that can be laid out on a horizontal surface. The essential thing is that it be horizontal. But I am not Mephistopheles, and I do not want to beckon or lure you anywhere. What I mean by all this is that a vertical line can reach upward from any point, from any "corner" on the surface of any culture, be it young, be it decrepit with age.

For me, however, culture in its truest sense is not a surface extending only horizontally, nor is it a vista of ruins or a plain strewn with bare bones. Culture, for me, is something sacred that not only keeps alive the memory of the external features of our ancestors but also of their inward and deepest motivations and experiences: a perennial memory, which lives on in those who partake of those motivations and prolong those experiences. These have been transmitted over the ages from generation to generation, and nothing of this message, since the first letter was inscribed on the tablet of the human spirit, shall be effaced. Seen in this light, culture is not only monumental but initiatory in character, enabling the servants of memory—which is indeed the ruler of all culture—to renew their forebears' experience. Thus do they receive the energy to initiate new beginnings, new feats. Memory is dynamic, generative. Oblivion is exhaustion, all motion arrested, inertia established. Like Nietzsche, however, we should examine ourselves closely to see whether we are not carrying within us the poisons of decay and "decadence."

What is decadence? The feeling of an underlying oneness with the central tradition of a high culture coupled with an arrogant and burdensome sense of being the last of a line. In other words, decadence is an enervated memory, its promotive capacity gone, without the power to enable us to partake in our forefathers' creative experience, no longer able to encourage creativity. It is the knowledge that prophecy has ceased, as the decadent Plutarch suggests in the title of his work on "Why the Oracles Cease to Give An-

27

swers." The spirit no longer speaks to decadent man with its customary voice; only the soul of times past speaks to him; his spiritual impoverishment makes him turn to the psyche alone, and he becomes a psychologist. Will he understand the words of Goethe's *Vermachtniss:* "Truth was discovered long ago, and ever since has cemented the community of higher minds. This old truth you must strive to grasp"?

To the psychologist this is just more psychology. At any rate, he suspects everything spiritual and objective of being psychological and subjective. Again some lines from Goethe come to mind: it is what Faust says about Wagner: "With avid hand he delves in the earth seeking the golden fruit, and rejoices when he finds a worm." Is this not reminiscent of our friend who yearns for the water of life and who in his psychological researches uncovers the futility of theorizing? He may be left to his demon; let the dead bury the dead. To believe him means to open one's spirit to mildew. Of course, this does not diminish our love, our tender pity for him, nor does it diminish his achievements as tragic gravedigger. For our part we shall believe in the life of the spirit, in sanctity and initiations, in the invisible saints who surround us and in a limitless host of struggling souls, we shall go bravely forward without a sidelong or backward glance, without measuring the distance we have come, without heeding the voices of fatigue and inertia and their talk of "poison in the bloodstream and exhaustion in the bones."

We can be joyous wayfarers on this earth without

leaving our native town, and become poor in spirit
without forgetting all we know. Long ago we recognized that the human understanding is a subordinate
tool, a servant of the will, apt to serve life's needs like
any other of the body's lower organs; and the theories
that permeate it, to use your words, can be given away
to others the way we give away useless books gath-
ering dust on our shelves. But mindful of Goethe's
"truth discovered long ago," let us inhale the life-giv-
ing essence of these theories and religions, their spirit
and logos and their energy. As carefree and inquisitive
as strangers eager to learn, let us wander past the row
upon row of altars and idols of monumental culture,
some forlorn and in disrepair, some restored and re-
furbished, stopping here and there, if we so wish, to
offer a sacrifice at those forgotten places where an
ever-blooming flower, invisible to others, has sprung
up from an ancient grave.

—V.I.

July 4th

VIII. *To V.I. Ivanov*

YOU are a siren, my friend, and your letter of yesterday is truly an enchantment. It was as if culture in person were cunningly enticing me with her riches while lovingly admonishing me not to forsake her. Yes, her voice is irresistible and, indeed, am I not one of her children?—not the prodigal son you have in mind, but, far more sadly, the son of a prodigal mother. Your diagnosis, however, dear doctor, is altogether mistaken. I had better express myself more clearly.

By no means do I wish to set mankind back to the mentality and customs of, say, the inhabitants of the Fiji Islands, nor do I wish to unlearn writing or banish the Muses. Neither do I dream of wild flowers in meadows. It seems to me that not even Rousseau, who caused a commotion throughout Europe with his dream, ever dreams of a *tabula rasa;* any such dream would be empty, absurd, and unappealing.

But this time you have put your finger on what is essentially at issue between us. Hitherto you had supposed that, bored with the products of culture, I was peevishly about to throw out the baby with the bath-water. Not so! I have been speaking of temptations of the spirit and of poison in the bloodstream and in life itself. I have been speaking precisely of the most pre-cious achievements to have come of thousands of years of experience, speaking of what you refer to as "the true initiations of our forefathers," speaking of objec-tive and immutable truth. This wellspring of spiritual life, I have been saying, is contaminated and no longer assures anything but death to those who drink thereof. What is at issue is the dynamic potential of discovered truth, its power to promote initiations of the spirit.

It is from memory, you say—after having called memory the ruler of all culture—that memory's ser-vants receive the energy to initiate new beginnings, new feats, renewing their forebears' experience.

Oh, if only this were so! It was so once, it isn't any-more. The light-bringing truths once upon a time re-vealed to ancestors have turned into mummies, fetishes; instead of bursting upon the spirit with the wonderfully excessive force of lightning, they bury the soul beneath a deepening rubble of moribund ideas. Objective truth is and yet is not. It exists in real-ity only as a way and a direction, but not as a known and assumed fact that can and must be got hold of, as Goethe maintains in the lines you cite to me. Life would not be worth living if it were true that "truth was discovered long ago." It is not the content of what our forefathers initiated that is precious, because the content of every discovered truth is relative and hence

31

to that degree false and ephemeral; what is precious is their methodology alone, if that is a suitable term in this context.

You better than anyone should know that every expression of truth is perforce symbolic, simply a gesture, a sound that brings us to attention and prompts us to turn to look in the direction from which it came. When you speak of truth as a source of unending initiation, you present human existence not as it is but just as I wish it were. I say the initiations that were the work of past times have become petrified, have changed into despotic values which tempt us, browbeat us, and end by reducing the individual spirit to passive and even voluntary submission, or, shrouding the spirit in fog, render us blind. But allow me to recall what I have written before on this head:

Everybody knew that Napoleon was not born an emperor. Any ordinary woman in the crowd watching him ride by during some great parade might have said to herself: "Now he is the Emperor who almost lost his personal name: he is the ruler of whole nations. But when he was in his swaddling clothes he was nothing to the world, only his mother's child." And I standing before a famous picture in a museum think the same thing: the artist painted it for himself, in the creative act it was inseparable from him—he was in the picture and the picture in him. Yet now the picture has been exalted into an objective value recognized universally.

Everything objective has its birthplace in the individual and originally belonged to him only. Whatever the value under discussion, its biography reveals the three phases Napoleon went through: at the outset it is of no account to the world, then it is a warrior and a leader on the battlefield, finally it is the ruler. Like Napoleon in Ajaccio, a value is free and true only in its earlier years when, unknown, it plays, grows and suffers in freedom, without attracting covetous interest. Only once was the whole fullness of *Hamlet* ever achieved: within Shakespeare. And all the truth of the Sistine *Madonna* with Raphael. Then the world enrolls these values for service in its everyday battles. The world has no use for their fullness. The world has detected in the value that special force with which its creator endowed it, the world would now exploit that force for its own needs: the world's relationship to the value is determined by greed, and greed always knows what it wants.

Once in general use, the value invariably becomes differentiated, disintegrating into components, into particular and special meanings; in the process its fullness and its essence go by the board. Just as the oak is necessary to man not in its natural state as a standing tree, but sawed up in pieces, so man prizes a value only when its essence has been fragmented, and many purposes can be served by its many parts. Finally, this utility itself becomes a generally accepted value, and the value is enthroned. Enthroned, the value is cold and cruel and in the course of time it petrifies and becomes a fetish. Gone is every trace of the freshness and exuberant strength it once radiated. The many ser-

33

vices it has rendered, noble and base! Somebody wanted a bucket, somebody else wanted the rain to fall, it gave satisfaction to one and all, confirming each in his selfish little truth. And now it lays down the law to the whole world, deaf to the individual plea. What was once alive and individual, what was once part and parcel of one man's blood and bone, has become an idol requiring the sacrifice of living people no different from what it itself was when it first appeared in the world. The emperor Napoleon and the painting enthroned in a museum are equally despotic.

Alongside fetish-values, which are tangible and concrete, there are vampire-values, the ones known as abstract values, not unlike legal persons in the sphere of values. They are bodyless and invisible, by means of abstraction they are distilled from concrete values, rather as the evaporation of water from the earth leads to a cloud in the sky. Through abstraction from a good many *Hamlets* and Sistine *Madonnas* a general value was arrived at: the value called Art. All the others were concocted likewise: Property, Morality, Church, Religion, and Nation and the State, Culture, and many more. They are all descended from the best blood of the most passionate human hearts. Each of them now has its own cult, its own priesthood and its own faithful. The priests speak pressingly to the masses about the "interests" and "needs" of the particular value they worship, demanding sacrifices necessary to its well being. The State thirsts for power, the Nation for unity, Industry for development, etc.; phantoms though they are, they effectively rule the world, and the more abstract a value, the more extensive and unsparing its demands. We could perhaps think of the last war as nothing but a hecatomb without precedent, which a number of conceptualized values that had got together proceeded to wring from Europe through the intermediary of their priests.

Nevertheless, every abstract value, however gluttonous, contains a lingering spark of divinity. By it, every individual can be affected; in it, perhaps unconsciously, every individual pays his respects to some ineradicable aspiration which he shares with all men. And the value's strength comes from this living feeling alone. When, for instance, I eat to satisfy my hunger, or put on clothing to cover my nakedness, or pray to God, these are petty articles of personal business, confined to me. Observe now how my personality is awarded a social status, how it is boosted into impersonal realms and, higher still, into the giddy reaches of suprapersonal principles. And now behold! my feeling of being just me has found a place within a complex and highly centralized hierarchical structure. Up around that little prayer there has now arisen a colossal edifice of Theology, Religion, the Church. What had been a need of my heart is declared my sacred duty. It has been taken from my hands as something precious and has been placed above me, anointed and my sovereign. The poor heart which gave vent to the prayer loves it still, as a mother loves her child within the tyrant he has become, but she weeps as she obeys his impersonal will. At last there comes a time when love overcomes submissiveness: the mother brings the tyrant down in order to retrieve her son. So it was that Luther with his ardent heart brought down the cult, the theology, the church of the Pope, with the aim of liberating simple faith, personal faith from a strait-jacketing system. The French Revolution made away with the mystique of the throne and instituted a more direct relationship between the people and authority. Another rebellion is now shaking the earth: the truth of labor and of individual possession is struggling to break free of centuries-old complications, of the abominable fetters of social and abstract ideas.

We have still a long way to go. Luther's Christianity, the Republic, and Socialism have brought mankind only halfway; conditions have still to be found under which individuality can be wholly individual once again, as it was originally.

But the past will not have been for nothing. Man will return to his beginnings richer, transformed, because his subjectivity, made into an objective and universal value, for many, many years flourished as eternal truth in that world above. What we are witnessing is a kind of phylogeny in reverse: having reached its apogee, the movement is now in the other direction, retracing the same path by which it ascended, stage by stage. With each revolution, you see, the old is reborn: the monarchy is ousted by a common council—parliament; parliamentarianism will be replaced by federation, an even earlier form, and on it will go until the original point of departure is reached. However, there is a new spirit in the old forms. In its ascent, the community was poor, chaotic, and closed; in descent it is both organized and universalized. The starting point to which all must return is individuality, individuality now enriched by all that it has acquired from its conquests. It will take centuries but faith will once again be personal and simple, work will again be individual creation and joyous, and possession will be intimate communion between man and object. But faith and the ideas of work and property will be immutable and sacred within the individual, and outside him those things themselves will be immeasurably richer, a single seed will have become a tree. The present task, I repeat, is to enable individuality to become individual once again—and at the same time to be experienced as universal. Man, like Mary, must be enabled to recognize in each of his manifestations both his child and God.

Values, though, are not everything. Values can be fought against; but how can we fight against poisons that culture has introduced into our blood and which have attacked the very sources of spiritual life? There are webs of thought, constructed out of age-old experience, and they are of steel. Gradually and surely they ensnare the mind. There are the tried and true pathways, the ruts in which thinking is overtaken by laziness. Along with routine thinking there are routines of conscience, routines of perception, there are cliches of sentiment and the innumerable clichés of speech.

They lie in wait for every least seed of thought or feeling, pounce upon it as though amorously, and lure it toward the commonplace. Lastly, there are the countless bits and pieces that result from knowledge, terrifying in their number and their inexorableness; they flood the mind and set up there as objective truth, without waiting for hunger to summon the few among them that could answer a real need. Beset on all sides, the constricted spirit withers, incapable either of appropriating them in some meaningful way or of expelling them. No, I am not speaking at all of freedom *from* theory. I am speaking of freedom of theory. To be more precise, of freedom, immediacy and freshness of contemplation—in order that the wisdom come down to us from the past not overbear the timid nor favor inertia nor obscure our horizon; in order that a new sensibility and a new species of thinking emerge, a sensibility and a thinking that will not immediately solidify in each of their achievements, but remain plastic forever, infinitely mobile. Only at this point will they appear, those light-hearted wayfarers you speak of, poor in spirit, carefree and inquisitive. You see no such wayfarer today, or if you do he is such only in appearance. Today nobody walks, like a stranger, *by* the altars and the idols. You too, my friend, without realizing it, sacrifice on many altars and unconsciously worship idols; how is that? Because the poison is in our bloodstream. It is not I who wish to pin humanity down to a horizontal plane. It is you who have written that "we shall go bravely forward without a sidelong or backward glance, without measuring the distance . . ." What I say is that individuality on this plane is the vertical line along which the new culture might ascend.

—M.G.

IX. *To M.O. Gershenzon*

THE dialogue between us is becoming difficult. It has sharpened into an argument—to my surprise, let me add. For you, dear friend, are a monologuist by nature. It is not possible to lead you onto the paths of dialectics; logic, in your eyes, is not a law. You are unconcerned by your contradictions; these, made up into a list, I could present to you the way bills are presented if propriety did not deter me from such an attack upon the inner, the *psychic* meaning of your confessions. But it seems to me that we did agree that truth must not become compulsive. So what is there left for me to do? To sing and play my pipe? "We piped unto you, and ye did not dance; we wailed, and ye did not mourn." Thus the children in the marketplace calling to their fellows; but we consider that we are not children anymore. "Prettily sung," you are likely to say to the singer, casting him a kind smile as you continue on your way.

"Enjoy your trip to the promised land!" is what I feel I should call after you, because that is what you are raving about, the promised land of vineyards and fig trees ("They shall sit each under his vine and under his fig tree," as it is written in the Bible), green pastures and cool springs, but exactly where it is and just what it is like—for it might possibly lie outside this phenomenal world—you do not seem to need to know provided you can get there (and we absolutely cannot fail to get there, that is the promised part about it) or at least sight it from Mount Nebo, because in it "shines the triple image of perfection." And you would not swap your nomadic restlessness and your thirst for cool water—the ancient thirst of those who wandered forty years in the desert—for the "fleshpots of Egypt" and Egypt's temples, pyramids and mummies and all the Egyptian wisdom and initiations. Like Moses, you have been introduced to this wisdom and these initiations and now your wish is to forget it all; you detest Egypt, you behold with loathing a mummified culture and a wisdom that does nothing for *your* thirst!

What a difference there is between you and Nietzsche whose burden (which is as alien to you as the whole of Egypt) you declined to try to take upon your shoulders, overladen as they already are by the burden of spiritual values and monuments. What would it profit you to make the perilous pilgrimage with him into the valley of the Sphinx whose singing riddle ("Who and what art thou, O stranger?" to which Oedipus answers, "A man") carries the sound of a different melody for each person who hears it? In the end, however, Nietzsche's problem is also your problem: culture and individuality, values, decadence or health, health especially. And in our cultural milieu today one can hardly imagine any initiation of individuality without the "initiate" (as the theosophists say) encountering Nietzsche as the "guardian of the gate." "Man is something which must be transcended," Nietzsche said, thereby testifying once again that the one path to the liberation of the individual is a path that takes him thither by way of heights and depths, proceeding along a vertical line. Again an obelisk, again a pyramid. "This may be! This may very well be," you say, dismissing the question in your haste to be off, for you have girded up your loins and your eyes are scrutinizing the wilderness prospect ahead, "but first I have to get out of here! Get away from Egypt!"

If for any length of time and to any extent you had been a Nietzschean you would be unable to ignore that in man, culture's camel-like beast of burden (the figure of speech is Nietzsche's, the pathos yours), lion's claws show through. You would have understood how the predator's elemental hunger speaks up in him, forcing him to tear apart some living thing and taste its blood. In the abstract language of the new Egypt and in the writings of its priests this living blood-filled thing is called "values." They are marvelously vital and long-lived, mankind, as you have said, having fed them upon its own blood, breathed into them the fire of its soul, though they now sit motionless upon their thrones like "graven images, or any likeness of any thing that is in heaven above, or that is in the earth beneath, or that is in the water under the earth." But Nietzsche is not only a breaker, a drinker of blood and a devourer of souls; he is also a legislator who, even before becoming the "youth" into whom, according to his prophecy, the lion must be transformed, shatters the tables of the ancient values in order to engrave new words upon new tables, *unque leonis.* To old Egypt he wants to give a new testament, wants, he says, to "transvaluate" that same pagan heritage. Thus he joins the company of the great molders of the ideal: first the iconoclast, the breaker of images, he becomes the artist who engenders them.

All very well—but your craving is for cool water, not for hot blood: rather than a predatory beast you are merely a wanderer in the desert; and when you reach Egypt, the inquisitorial tribunal of soothsayers would probably look upon you not as a destroyer but as a sower of suspicions, doubts, trouble; while as for legislating, you have no propensity in that direction; and, actually, no transvaluating appears to you to be called for, since between the going values and your own there may be no basic discrepancy—still, for some reason, you cannot leave the former alone, and must begin with their supposed dethronement and abolition. Perhaps you feel that values cannot be revived unless they are first killed, that to be immortal a god must survive the test of death. I would say that you are moved by a deep and secret impulse diametrically opposed to the impulses which over the ages regularly determined the shaping of idols throughout what the

Scriptures call the pagan world. The genius of paganism projected its finest part into a transcendental image or into an invisible but transcendental idea—an impalpable image—and objectified its highest part as a symbol, an effigy, or an idol. Even "upon the shoals of time" (to use your expression) in the century of Kant and the locking and sealing of the spirit by reflection into the solitary cell of individual personality, it sought to save "the idea" as "the regulative idea" in the rational consciousness of man. You do not realize it, but you are a typical representative of an equally ancient and iconoclastic line whose impulse is to absorb the idea in the halflight of the unconscious. You have no use for "the regulative idea"—transcendent or immanent, it remains an idea—; it is oppressive to you; it is a regulative instinct that you need. You neither see God nor wish God to be in the visible sky or in man's invisible skies; you want Him to be in the living creature's very soul, in the breath it breathes, in the pulse of its blood. A very ancient way of thinking, I repeat, a way of thinking quite as ancient as the hieroglyphics of Egypt, seconds you in this. I once wrote some lines about primitive man who did not fear death as we fear it—

> Ancient man, you are mightier than we
> Because you did not lower your youthful gaze
> Before inexorable fate.

Did he believe in the immortality of the soul? If so, this faith brought him neither comfort nor hope;

rather, it must have been for him cause for the greatest gloom.

> Yet while despair secretly crushed
> His mind, and the darkness of the Hospitable
>   Temple
> Filled his dream with dread—
> In his sinews ripened sunlike strength
> And as it fed his veins with joyous life,
> 'I am immortal!' sang forth his blood.

Is this not true belief in immortality? The conclusion to be drawn from all you have been saying is that the first true and perfect ideal is the instinct, with its immanent theology (because it is in accord with nature). That, I am certain, is why you have no desire to make use of the freedom of speculation that you nevertheless demanded: faithful to yourself, you begin your correspondence with me by declaring that "these are things"—God and immortality—"about which we should not talk or even think."

Pray forgive my typological investigations of your psychic and intellectual make-up: *amico licet.* But how else can one reply to a man who, unwilling to employ the devices of persuasion (with the exception of one—probably the most forceful—: the beauty of words) simply insists: *hoc volo*—such is my will, such is my thirst and *ut sentio sitioque ita sapio.* We have still to investigate the sources of this will and the nature of this thirst. But for such an inquiry to be sufficient, we would also have to locate the will as an essential phenomenon connected with the broad change we are undergoing at present.

What then is happening in our time? Is it the doing away with cultural values in general? Or are they disintegrating after first having fallen into partial or complete disuse? Or is some transvaluation of former values now afoot? Whatever the answer, the fact is that the values of yesterday are being profoundly shaken, and I would have to include you among those who rejoice in this earthquake, since according to you the old Egypt must be destroyed lest "the image of perfection" which once lighted the cradle of its creations remain forever buried inside the pyramids. However, it appears that history is not unfolding in conformance with your prescriptions, but persists in wanting to remain history, possibly only a new page in the annals of cultured Egypt.

Leaving aside the accidental, the unforeseeable, the irrational in the course of events, let us focus upon the state of our contemporaries' minds. Anarchistic tendencies have lost much ground: they seem to be little more than a by-product and correlate of the bourgeois order. What is called the conscious proletariat is standing firmly for cultural continuity. The aim of the struggle is not to do away with the values of the cultural past; the great thing being fought for is the revitalization of everything from the past that has a permanent validity—an urgent and supreme task of transvaluation, to be carried out as soon as possible. The lion who has risen up from the lower depths and

46

sprung upon the established values has not emerged from the camel and he is more than a beast of prey; he is what Nietzsche saw him to be, the lion-man, to whom "no human trait is alien." And at present, as Nietzsche foretold, he is breaking the old tables of the Law and attempting to scratch new laws on new tables, *unque leonis*. While I believe he will spoil no end of handsome slabs of marble and bronze plates in the course of his efforts, I also believe that some perhaps unique but ineffaceable trace of the lion's claws will show forever upon the monuments of our own "ancient Egypt." At all events, the question here is not the content of the new Twelve Tables but the method used to deal with values.

The method of the revolution that has driven our two weary and rundown selves into a municipal rest home where we talk about health, is a primarily social and historical method, a political method; a method that is not utopian or anarchical or otherwise stamped by individualism. It is the method of those who stay put where they are, not of those who cut and run, of the settled rather than the nomadic sort—and at present, let me interject, we are addressing none of the questions of spiritual ascent or growth along vertical lines, when rights and duties all yield in importance to the principle of individuality, of the human individual, unique and irreplaceable. But, here, we are once more approaching its sacred precinct.

I maintain that both Mount Nebo and the Promised Land itself are to be found in the spirit that animates individuality. You set individuality and value in opposition, as when you compare the mother who raised the infant Napoleon with the same woman who now, estranged from her son, contemplates him enthroned in a glory so magnificent and so coldly excluding that she sees only the negation of her past life and love. Well, my friend, the profoundest aspiration of the human will was well expressed by the Pharaohs, whose chief preoccupation in life was to build themselves a fitting tomb. In addition to self-preservation, every living thing seeks self-revelation, certain in its depths that this must lead to self-exhaustion, self-destruction, and death—and also, perhaps, to eternal remembrance.

The desire to leave behind something lasting of oneself, to convert life into a monument of value, the desire to disappear in order to survive forever in the living cult of the principle that animates us, that is the source of the ancient obsession with valor, with *arete*, which was what the Hellenes and Dorians called the categorical imperative of active virtue. Mankind's initiation into the supreme mysteries revealed to it another aspect of the seeking for death in order to live: on the human plane and on the divine plane as well, truth and love and beauty tend towards the eucharistic: "eat my flesh and drink my blood, for my flesh is meat indeed, and my blood is drink indeed."

So it is not the mother of Bonaparte at the foot of her son's throne, but Mary at the foot of the Cross who symbolizes the heart before the great truth of the universal value. That value must be crucified, placed in a coffin and covered with a stone and sealed fast in the tomb, so that the heart may see it rise again on the third day.

At this point, unexpectedly, your voice joins mine and out of our love and common hope we prophesy together, not in my words but in what you have said about this, that the craving of the human heart shall be satisfied and the will of the spirit fulfilled, that individuality will become individual once again, and at the same time it will be experienced as universal, and that "Man, like Mary, must be enabled to recognize in each of his manifestations both his child and God."

—V.I.

July 17, 1920

X. *To V.I. Ivanov*

IT amuses me how you treat me the way a doctor treats a patient: my illness saddens you as a friend, frightens you as a member of society and even vexes you. You began everything with a wrong diagnosis and now you are surprised that your treatment is not successful. When you have been unable to conjure my feeling away with historical arguments and rational demonstrations, you blame my obstinacy for your failure. This works about as well as a father trying to warn his son that the girl he loves will never make him happy. Or as repeating to a man who is thirsty that he should not drink, that he is better off suffering because his thirst is not a real thirst and will soon pass. I am not at all unwilling to discuss your many arguments, and can counter them with at least one that, methodologically speaking, replies to them all. Heraclitus said: "It is hard to fight against impulse; whatever it wishes, it buys at the expense of the soul." In the same vein, I would suggest that when historical reason passes judgment on culture, it is naturally predisposed to glorify it. If you find it necessary to inquire into the nature of my thirst, I have as much right to examine the cause of your satiety.

And now I come to what you have to say about Nietzsche. You are again in error, my good doctor. I read little of Nietzsche, he did not suit my taste; and it is clear to me now that my "pathos," as you call it, has nothing to do with his. Unwell himself, he found it possible to forecast the sickness of culture and on the strength of this prognosis, to prescribe laws to the future. The man of culture is to beget a lion, and in its turn the lion is to beget a child: therefore "Become lions as soon as you can, be bold, tear others to pieces." After the hideous war of 1914–1918 it has become difficult to speak of the birth of lions. The war showed that a bloodthirsty wild beast had ripened inside the cultured and civilized man of our time; this creature being anything but a lion, I have little hope indeed that it will bring forth a child. No, it is not for us to compose laws for the future. It will be enough if we are able to recognize our illness and our need to be cured—that is, in itself, the beginning of a possible recovery. I find nothing strong in Nietzsche except his cries of pain.

All through your arguments I seem to hear one continual note: a pious respect for history. You are loath to find it at fault; whatever it has created, that you devoutly accept; and my rebellion galls you. Yet in one of your earlier letters you spoke with conviction of the original fall of man, very certainly referring to the sin of schism and of withdrawal into closed individualities centered upon the self. You admit, then, that man's will is in some measure free to fashion its existence in one way or another. Why need you be upset when I say that our contemporary culture is the result of error, that modern man has taken the wrong turn and is inextricably lost in a wilderness? No doubt about it, history has been rational at every point, meaning that everything that has happened can be explained. But an explanation is not an evaluation. Required by an inherent law to defend itself, the deer developed antlers to defeat or intimidate its enemies, yet in some species those antlers attained such proportions that the animal could no longer flee through the forest and those species are now extinct. Is it not the same with culture? Is there not a parallel to be drawn between our "values" and those antlers? They began as a result of individual adaptation, then became a characteristic feature of the race, finally through excessive growth they turn into a tormenting burden that can even be fatal for the individual.

Yes, you are right: your logic is not law for me. At no point in history is history's truth consecrated. It is a truth forever in the process of emerging, and is created, measured and verified in each individual. My own individuality having tested this truth by the feel of it, says to it: You feel to me like a lie. I cannot worship you. To Perun I say: you are a wooden idol, you are not God. God I feel as invisible and present everywhere. You however wish me to think that this statue is a symbol of my deity and that once I grasp everything it stands for it will entirely replace God for me.

52

Despite the interesting and profound things you tell me about its symbolic nature (I am ready to listen endlessly to words as persuasive as yours!) the appearance of the thing revolts me, its disturbing effect upon me is incoercible. I remember all the sacrifices we have made to it in the past, I think of the others I shall be obliged to offer following the daily instructions of its priests. Bloody, weighty sacrifices. No! This is not God. *My* God is an invisible God, He does not exact, He does not affright, He does not crucify. He is my life, my movement, my freedom, my intimate will.

This is what I meant when I said that my thirst cannot be quenched by the warm and high-flavored brews of current philosophy, art, and poetry, that my thirst can be quenched only with cold spring water. And the water of life has vanished today: all the springs have disappeared inside reservoirs, their water is imprisoned within endless miles of pipes, is filtered, sterilized; in cities this half-dead liquid is further processed; what we get to drink is either boiled water or queer beverages made up of all sorts of things, with strange colors, flavors and odors. Surrounded by these flagons of dense and tepid philosophy, hot and aromatic poetry, it is easy to die of thirst before finding a mouthful of fresh water. Forgive me this lengthy metaphor; but we have been having hot weather, and I find no refreshment anywhere. I continue to drink and drink the warm boiled water, I have drunk everything that was in our carafe, and my thirst is still there. Little wonder if it has found its way into my writing.

I remember a summer day, a day like today, many

years ago, when I drank from a spring in the woods near Kusnovo. It was shady and cool there and drinking the clear clean water was sheer delight. And how can I—who because fate would so have it, because culture so ordered, am living in the city, resting in a rest home, in a poorly ventilated room with a window looking out upon a wall, where all I have is awful boiled water to drink and swarms of flies to swat at—how can I forget that green woods and coolness exist somewhere, and not long for them? How can I? And one more point, let me underscore it:

> If only our hard fate
> Would spare our children and not recur. . . .

My feeling is not affected by the logic of abstract thought; nor is it ready to knuckle under before the logic of history, with its superstitious veneration of history. You invoke against me not only the rationality inherent in the past but also, as your clinching argument, its continuation manifest in the events of our own day.

You bid me open my eyes to the revolution now going forward; its watchword is not the scrapping of the values of past culture, its design is to put them into the possession of everybody; it is not a rebellion against culture, it is a struggle to preserve it, and, as you say, "the conscious proletariat is standing firmly for cultural continuity." Yes; but what of it? What we see is the proletariat taking this hoard of values out of the hands of the few and into its own. At the same time we have no idea what the proletariat sees in them or has in mind to do with them. In them might it not see only an instrument of its timeless oppression, something it has no wish to own but needs to remove from the hands of its former masters? Or would it be that under the impact of public education the proletariat has come to place some store by culture and supposes its values worth having? Who can tell? Once the proletariat has got hold of these treasures, it may well realize that they are nothing more than chains and rubbish, and, disappointed and angry, toss them out and set to work creating different values of its own. Still another possibility is that it will lift these cultural values onto its own shoulders and carry them forward, assuming the burden of the cultural heritage in good faith. But if the old values continue in currency among the proletariat, the proletariat will infuse a new spirit into them and before long their molecular structure will have changed to the point where they are unrecognizable.

It is quite possible—and this in fact is my actual belief—that, at this moment, in its effort to gain possession of these values, the proletariat is mistaken. It feels it needs them as such; in truth they are of no use to it except as stepping-stones to something new. We have a curious way of deceiving ourselves about what we are after. Man creates the airplane, his thoughts focussed upon its usefulness: it will enable him to cover great distances in less time, or get the stock market news faster from New York to Chicago, but he does not know that the inspiration to build himself wings proceeds from other longings than to satisfy his earthly needs. He does not know that his profounder ambition is to break free from the earth and to soar above it, that his dream of flight to other worlds has turned into faith in that possibility, that the airplane is merely the rudimentary first stage in the fulfillment of this dream rooted amongst his most underlying intuitions: the day will come when I will fly for ever and disappear into the ether without a trace. Likewise did ancient man strike his first spark from flint, moved by a sense that darkness is not inevitable and that it was within his power to overcome it; today, night becomes day at the touch of a switch. In the conscious intention the genuine goal is not spelled out; the spirit conceives goals all by itself, and advises consciousness only piecemeal: a first step will be in this direction, a second step in that other, and so on. Towards what the path is leading only the spirit knows; and this is why consciousness feels deceived after every step. Wundt's terms for this phenomenon is heterogeneity of goals: the goal that consciousness sets on the path of realization is shifted or replaced by another, totally alien to the first, this process being repeated on and on, so that a path which we intended to be straight and short becomes sinuous and longer. Thus does the spirit imperceptibly but imperiously steer the walker, guiding his feet toward its own dream, unknown to reason. What we now see in this revolution tells us nothing of the long-range plan and purpose for which the spirit brought it into being.

—M.G.

XI. *To M.O. Gershenzon*

DEAR friend, have we not compromised ourselves enough already, each in his own way, I with my mysticism and you with your anarchistic utopianism and cultural nihilism, as the "compact majority" (Ibsen's term) of today's committees and political meetings would define and condemn our two attitudes? Ought not each of us to retire to his corner and keep still there? "How shall the heart express itself? How shall 'the other' understand? How shall he know what makes you live? Every uttered thought is a lie." I would not wish to abuse this melancholy confession of Tiuchev's; I prefer to think that it expresses not an eternal truth but the lie fundamental to this period of cultural disarray, this age that is powerless to generate a true community of consciousness, an age now being visited by the penultimate consequences of the ancient sin of "individuation," which has poisoned all of human culture and all of the historical life of mankind. We strain every day and every hour to stem this fatal tide by the creative process carried on in small cults and in large—and every cult is catholic so long as it is alive, even if the communicants are but three in number, or two—and catholicity blazes up briefly and then dies out again because the thousand-headed hydra of culture, at never-ending odds with itself, cannot become a harmonious cult.

But in our thirst for unity we must not let ourselves be tempted into making compromises, as for example establishing an outward and fictitious bond, one in which the roots of consciousness, the vital threads of our spiritual being, have not knit into one common fabric. In the depth of depths, at a level profounder than we can fathom, we are all linked together into a universal system of blood circulation feeding into the single heart of all mankind. But we must take care lest we be led into substituting an image of our making for the sacred reality underneath. You and I do not have a cult in common.

You feel that oblivion liberates and revives, whilst cultural memory enslaves and kills. I, on the other hand, believe that memory liberates whilst oblivion enslaves and kills. I speak of the road climbing upward and you reply that the wings of the spirit have become too heavy to take flight. "Let us go away!" is your cry, to which I say: "There is no place to go—the repositioning of a body on a given plane changes neither the nature of the plane nor that of the displaced body." Once I wrote:

> To you, old ancestral trees
> And crowded burial grounds;
> To us, free open spaces—
> That was the judgment of Beauty.

Endless betrayal,
A new camp every day.

But then the truthful Muse compelled the poet for all his rebellion against cultural tradition, to add these lines:

The wanderer's illusion
Of inescapable imprisonment.

O, for the sake of the cult we ought to renounce the ancient sites and the ancestral trees:

Brothers, let us depart for the twilight of the sa-
cred groves . . .
The staff of exile is light to the children of gods,
The flowering thyrsus of new love.

Broad is the flowering earth and there are many clear glades upon it:

. . . they await our searching lips
And the dithyrambic unison of our feet. . . .

It will be so, even if there are no signs that this great hour has arrived. When it does, culture will be transformed into a cult of God and of the Earth. And memory will have wrought this miracle, mankind's primal memory. Essentially, culture is multiform, just as is eternity, just as is human individuality in its structure.

Seas are moving within the deep sea, some to
dawns, others to sunsets;

> Above, the waves tend toward noon, below, to-
> ward midnight;
> Many currents run in the streams of the dark
> deep,
> And in the purple ocean roll underwater rivers.

As in the ocean so in our culture hidden currents exist that convey us toward the very earliest sources of life. There will be an age of great and joyous home-coming, a mighty return, when fresh springs will burst forth between ancient headstones and roses will bloom from forgotten graves. To hasten the coming of that day we must press steadily forward; a halt or a retreat would only slow the closing of the circle of eternity.

Most of us Russians have always been prone to take to our heels. Our impulse is to run and not look back. Running away from a difficulty is a solution I am res-olutely against. I have said that the culture of Egypt is as alien to you as Nietzsche's *élan vital*. To almost all our "intelligentsia"—taking the term in its strict sense of a social and historical category—Egypt is alien and culture is slavery. You are flesh of the flesh and bone of the bone of our intelligentsia, your scuffling with them notwithstanding. For myself, I can hardly be in-cluded among them, being half a son of the Russian land, but banished from it, and half a foreigner, a dis-ciple of Saïs where race and tribe are forgotten.

To become simple—*oprostit'sya*—that's the magic word with our intelligentsia, where all their uprooted condition is plaintively expressed. By becoming simple, they imagine, you get your roots back in the earth, you get a leg to stand on. Among them was Leo Tolstoy, for whom you must feel an affinity. Dostoevski, of an altogether different breed, would logically repel you. He did not want to become simple. But what he wrote about the healing influence of gardens upon the ills of communal life and about the education of children in the great gardens of the future, and of factories themselves standing amid gardens, these were not dreams at all, they constituted a program of social action—spiritually right and historically correct. To become simple is treason, oblivion, to turn tail, the reaction of fatigue and fear. The idea of becoming simple makes as little sense in cultural life as it would in mathematics—where "simplification" is a formal operation for reducing multiple complexities to more perfect forms of simplicity.

Simplicity in this sense is incompletion overcome by completion, imperfection by perfection; in this sense, simplicity is an achievement of the very highest. The road to simplicity goes by way of complexity. Complexity is conquered, simplicity attained, not by running away from this or that country or these or those surroundings, but by ascent. Ascent from wherever you are. In every place—and I repeat this again and again—there is a Bethel, in the center of every horizon a Jacob's ladder. Such is the way of true freedom, active and creative. The freedom stolen through oblivion is empty and null. Those who forget their kin are fugitive slaves or freedmen perhaps, but not free-born. Culture is the cult of ancestors, it is also—and this is somehow understood even nowadays—their resurrection. Mankind's direction is toward an ever keener self-awareness of man as "a forgotten god unmindful of what he is." Man has trouble remembering his first-born condition; the savage has forgotten it. The philosophy of culture my Prometheus expounds is *my* philosophy:

> . . . . to trade,
> To engage in art, wage war, to calculate,
> And to rule and to be a slave—so that
> In the noise of days, in cares, in lust,
> In dreams one might forget the direct and whole
> Freedom of being. While the savage
> Will wander in the empty places,
> Despondent. . . .

Neither the savage nor the man whose becoming "simple" under the spell of oblivion left him like a savage, can find joy in his empty freedom; both are sullen and dejected. There is but one way not to be a "gloomy visitor upon the dark earth": to die in the flames of the spirit on fire. *Dixi.*

—V.I.

July 15, 1920

XII. *To V.I. Ivanov*

YOU are angry and that is a bad sign. Irritated by my obtuseness, you are now classifying me among the "self-simplifiers" who have "forgotten their kin," you even label me a member of the "intelligentsia" (while you, O shrewd friend of mine, reserve a flattering title for yourself: son of the Russian land! and disciple of Saïs to boot!). But what irritates you most is my obstinately maintained *sic volo*—and refusal to argue. Do I refuse to argue? Why no, I argue with you all the time! Thus, for instance, in your last letter you make a pair of assertions: first, that the ultimate development of culture will bring us back to the original sources of life: we need only go forward with perseverance and at the end of the road we shall see the light shining, "fresh springs will burst forth between ancient headstones and roses will bloom from forgotten graves"— that is, an at present worthless culture will in the final stages of its decay retrieve its pristine state. My answer to this is that I don't believe it, and see no reason for thinking it. Only a miracle turns a fallen woman into Mary Magdalene. But that is what you count on, the spontaneous evolution of culture.

But the cheerfulness of this forecast is not extended to your second proposition, that every man should overcome culture by fiery death in the flames of the spirit. You cannot have it both ways: if culture through its own development leads us unerringly back to God, I, an individual, need not put myself out; I can peacefully continue my business as usual, present my lectures on the economic development of England in the Middle Ages, construct a railroad between Tashkent and the Crimea, look for a way to improve long-range artillery or to manufacture a better poison gas. In fact, I am even duty-bound to do so in order that culture proceed along its appointed path, in order to speed its longed-for consummation. In this case the fiery death of individuality not only serves no purpose, it is positively detrimental because an individuality gone up in flames to resurrection means one less worker on the cultural front. In this connection I shall remind you of your own verses:

> He who has known the anguish of earth's phe-
> nomena
> Also has know their beauty

and over and above that

> He who has known the beauty of phenomena
> Also has known the Hyperborean dream;
> While gently lulling quietude
> and fullness in his heart
> He calls for azure skies and emptiness. . . .

64

Precisely: "he calls for azure skies and emptiness." He will promptly stop preparing lectures, submit no further reports to the scientific society he belongs to, may even never again set foot upon its premises. And there is the fact that "fiery death in the spirit" is as rare a thing as the transformation of a prostitute into a saint. How can you claim that I do not argue? You can see that I am arguing with might and main.

But I have no argument with those lines of yours. You too, I gather, once experienced my anguish and my thirst—but then quieted down and talked all that away with sophisms about the ultimate transformation of culture or the at all times available possibility of personal salvation through "death in the flames." No indeed, we do not have a common cult, so long as you persist in your devout acceptance of all history. But there is something else that we have in common, as our friendship over all these years bears out.

I live a strangely double life. From childhood I have been in contact with European culture, I have bathed in its spirit; not only have I become thoroughly familiar with it, but there is much in it that I love. I love what I think of as its cleanliness and comfort; I love science, the arts, poetry, Pushkin; I feel at home in the cultural family, I love talking about cultural matters with my friends, with all and sundry, the themes we discuss and the methods of developing them interest me genuinely. In this regard I am with you: we have a common cult of service in the cultural marketplace, we have habits in common and a common language. This is my daytime life.

However, in the depths of my consciousness I lead another life. For many years I have heard a secret inner voice telling me, urgently, incessantly: *"This is not it, this is not it!"* In me another will backs off uneasily from culture, from everything being said and done around me, finding all of it boring and futile, like a turmoil of phantoms battling in a void. This will knows another world, perceives another life such as are not now upon the earth, but which will be and perforce must be, for genuine reality cannot otherwise be embodied at last; and this inner voice I recognize as the voice of my genuine self. I live like a foreigner adapted to a country that is not his own, liked by the natives and liking them in return, concerned for their welfare and exerting myself willingly in its behalf, suffering when they suffer, rejoicing when they rejoice. But I know that I am a foreigner, and in secret I miss the fields of my homeland, its different seasons, the different odor of its flowers in the springtime and the different speech of the women there.

Where is my homeland? I shall never lay eyes upon it, I shall die in a foreign place. And how passionately I long for it sometimes! At those times I have no more need of railroads and international politics; discussions of philosophical systems, my friends quarreling about a transcendent or an immanent God—all empty stuff, it seems to me, or worse than empty, blocking my view, like dust hanging over a road. But just as this stranger in a foreign land will feel a sudden thrill upon recognizing something of his homeland in the colors of a sunset or in the perfume of a flower and be profoundly moved, so do I even here feel the beauty and solace of the promised world. I feel it in the fields and in the woods, in the singing of birds and in the peasant behind his plow, in the eyes of children and on occasion in their words, in the ineffably kind smiles of women, in the compassion of man for man, in forthright and noble simplicity, in the glow suffusing certain words or an unexpected line of poetry that pierces the darkness like lightning at night, in many other things as well, in suffering above all. All these I shall find in my homeland too, because homeland is the flowering of these flowers, buried here beneath a marshy, coarse, vapid vegetation.

You, my friend, are in your native land, your heart is here, where your house is, that sky above this earth is yours. Your spirit is not split in two and I am fascinated by this integrity which, whatever its origin, is also a flower native to that land, our common land of the future. And that is what makes me think that in the house of our Father one abode is set aside for you and me, while here, on earth, the two of us stubbornly sit each in his corner, arguing about culture.

—M.G.

July 19th

The design of this book is the work of
Edmund Helminski, of Brattleboro, Vermont.
The typesetting has been by American–Stratford Graphic
Services, Inc.,
also of Brattleboro, Vermont.
The printing and binding are by
McNaughton & Gunn, Inc., Ann Arbor, Michigan.